My Secret Unicorn

Stronger Than Magic

Linda Chapman

Illustrated by Biz Hull

PUFFIN BOOKS

PUFFIN BOOKS

Published by the Penguin Group

Penguin Books Ltd, 80 Strand, London WC2R 0RL, England
Penguin Putnam Inc., 375 Hudson Street, New York, New York 10014, USA
Penguin Books Australia Ltd, 250 Camberwell Road, Camberwell, Victoria 3124, Australia
Penguin Books Canada Ltd, 10 Alcorn Avenue, Toronto, Ontario, Canada M4V 3B2
Penguin Books India (P) Ltd, 11 Community Centre, Panchsheel Park,
New Delhi – 110 017, India
Penguin Books (NZ) Ltd, Cnr Rosedale and Airborne Roads, Albany,
Auckland, New Zealand
Penguin Books (South Africa) (Pty) Ltd, 24 Sturdee Avenue,
Rosebank 2196, South Africa

Penguin Books Ltd, Registered Offices: 80 Strand, London WC2R 0RL, England

www.penguin.com

First published 2003

026

Text copyright © Working Partners Ltd, 2003
Illustrations copyright © Biz Hull, 2003
Created by Working Partners Ltd, London W6 0QT
All rights reserved

The moral right of the author and illustrator has been asserted

Set in 14.25 /21.5pt Bembo

Made and printed in England by Clays Ltd, St Ives plc

British Library Cataloguing in Publication Data
A CIP catalogue record for this book is available from the British Library

ISBN-13: 978-0-14-131345-0

www.greenpenguin.co.uk

My Secret Unicorn

Stronger Than Magic

As she reached the
paddock, she saw Twilight still
lying where she had left him. His nose
was resting heavily on the ground, his eyes
were closed. 'Twilight!' Lauren cried out.
Twilight's ears flickered and he half-raised his
head. He looked exhausted. Lauren scrambled
over the gate and raced across the grass. Throwing
herself down on the ground beside him, she
touched his neck. 'Twilight!' she
gasped. 'What's the matter? You look
really ill!'

For Bramble – my own Buddy
– you loved life so much.
I miss you every single day.

CHAPTER

One

'I love this place,' Lauren Foster whispered as she sat on Twilight's warm back. Fireflies danced around them, lighting up the dusky shadows of the peaceful forest glade.

Moonlight shone on Twilight's silvery horn as he nodded. 'Me too.'

Lauren patted him. She could hardly believe how lucky she was. Most of the time, Twilight looked like any ordinary grey pony, but when she said the words of the Turning Spell, he transformed into a magical unicorn and they flew to places like this secret glade in the woods.

'When we're here, I feel like anything could happen,' Lauren said, looking round at the unusual pinky-grey rocks.

'That's because it's a special place,' Twilight told her. 'There's magic in the air.' He snorted softly. 'Shall we stay here or shall we fly some more?'

Lauren glanced at her watch. 'We should really go home.'

Lauren's parents had no idea that Twilight was a unicorn. At the moment,

they just thought she was outside in his paddock, feeding him.

'I could use my unicorn powers to see whether they're worrying,' Twilight suggested. 'If they aren't, we could stay out a little longer.'

'That's a great idea,' Lauren replied.

Twilight trotted over to one of the unusual rocks at the side of the clearing. As a unicorn, he had many magical powers. One of them allowed him to use the rocks of rose quartz to see what was happening anywhere else in the world. Touching his horn to the surface of one, he said, 'Granger's Farm!'

There was a bright purple flash and mist started to swirl. As it cleared, an image of Lauren's home – Granger's Farm – appeared in the rock. Lauren slid off Twilight's back to look more closely. She could see Twilight's paddock, the surrounding fields filled with cows, her bedroom window, her mum's car . . .

'Lauren's mum and dad,' Twilight said to the rock.

The picture wobbled and suddenly Mr and Mrs Foster appeared. They were talking, but all Lauren could hear was a faint buzz. Tucking her long, fair hair behind her ears, she leaned closer to the rock. The buzz turned into voices.

'Is Lauren still outside with Twilight?' she heard her dad say.

Lauren tensed, but to her relief her mum spoke calmly.

'She is, but don't worry. She knows to be in by bedtime. She just likes spending as much time with him as possible,' Mrs Foster said, smiling. 'It's one of the best things about having moved to the country. Lauren and Max can have so much more freedom. If we were still in the city . . .'

Lauren saw her dad take her mum's hand. 'Moving here was the best thing we ever did,' he said.

Lauren sat back on her heels. 'It's OK,' she said to Twilight. 'I think we're safe for a while.'

'Shall we do some flying then?' Twilight said eagerly.

'In a minute,' Lauren said. She was enjoying looking at her family. 'Can I have a look at Max first?'

'All right,' Twilight said obligingly. 'Max!' he said.

The picture focused to show Max,

Lauren's six-year-old brother. He was
playing in his bedroom with his Bernese
mountain dog puppy, Buddy.

Lauren could tell from the way he was
holding a dog treat in his hand that he
was trying to get Buddy to sit.

She grinned at Twilight. 'Max and Buddy
are starting dog-training classes
tomorrow.' She watched the picture for a
few more seconds. It was fun not being
seen. 'Let's have a look at Mel now,' she
said to Twilight. 'Just quickly.'

Mel Cassidy was Lauren's neighbour
and one of her best friends. Twilight
murmured Mel's name and the picture
changed to show Mel sitting in her
bedroom with her mum. Mrs Cassidy
had her arm round Mel's shoulders.

'Mel's crying!' Lauren said in alarm.
She started to lean forward and then
stopped. Listening to her own family
was one thing, but somehow listening in
on a friend talking to her mum didn't

seem right. 'I don't know if we should listen,' she said doubtfully.

'But perhaps if we know what's wrong, we can help,' Twilight pointed out.

Lauren hesitated for a moment. She and Twilight were good at helping people in trouble. That's why unicorns came to live in the human world – to use their magical powers to do good deeds with their human owners. She looked at the picture in the rock. Mel looked really upset. Quickly, Lauren made up her mind. 'OK, but we'll only listen for a second,' she said.

Lauren and Twilight leaned closer.

'It's not fair,' she heard Mel say. 'I just can't do it, Mum. I've asked Mr Noland to explain twice now and I still don't get it!'

'You'll just have to ask Mr Noland to go through it again,' Mrs Cassidy said gently.

Lauren frowned in surprise. Mr Noland was their class teacher. What could be upsetting Mel?

'But then Lauren and Jessica will think I'm really dumb!' Mel cried.

'I'm sure they won't,' Mrs Cassidy said, hugging her. 'They're your friends.'

'But they can do fractions. It's just me who can't!' Mel said.

Fractions! Lauren sat back and the voices faded to a buzz again.

'Fractions?' Twilight said, sounding puzzled. 'What are they?'

'They're something we're doing
in maths,' Lauren answered.

'So it's nothing serious then,' Twilight
said in relief.

'Well, I don't know.' Lauren hesitated.
'If Mel's upset by it, then it is serious.
She seems to think Jessica and I will
laugh at her.' She shook her head. 'But
we'd never do that. We don't care if
she can do fractions or not. She's our
friend.' She chewed a fingernail. 'Poor
Mel,' she said softly. 'I wish I could help
her.'

Twilight looked doubtful. 'I don't think
any of my magic powers can help people
do maths.'

'I guess not,' Lauren said. 'It looks like

this is one problem I'll have to solve on my own.'

Twilight touched his horn to the rock. With a purple flash the picture disappeared. 'Let's go flying now,' he said.

Lauren didn't need any more encouragement. She vaulted on to Twilight's warm back. Taking two strides, he leapt upwards into the sky.

The wind whipped against Lauren's face and her hair blew out behind her as they swooped through the air before finally flying back to Granger's Farm.

'So, how are you going to help Mel?' Twilight asked her as they landed.

'I'm not sure yet,' Lauren replied. 'But I'll try to think of something by tomorrow.' She hugged him and said the Undoing Spell.

There was a purple flash and suddenly Twilight was no longer a unicorn but a small grey pony.

'Good night, Twilight,' Lauren whispered.

Twilight whickered softly and, giving him one last hug, Lauren hurried into the house.

CHAPTER
Two

'Lauren! You're going to be late for school!' Mrs Foster called up the stairs the next morning.

Lauren pulled a brush through her hair and hurried downstairs. School mornings were always a rush. As she ran into the kitchen, she almost fell over Buddy.

'Sit, Buddy! Buddy, sit!' Max was saying.

Seeing Lauren, Buddy leapt up in delight. Lauren tickled his ears. 'Hey, boy,' she said.

'Buddy! Come here and sit!' Max commanded sternly as the puppy gambolled around Lauren's legs.

Buddy crouched down with his front legs and stuck his bottom playfully in the air. 'Woof!' he barked, before bounding off wildly around the kitchen.

'He's going to be just great at obedience classes, Max,' Lauren teased as Buddy skidded to a halt too late and cannoned into the fridge door. 'He'll be bottom of the class.'

'He won't!' Max cried. 'Mum!' He turned to their mum. 'He won't, will he?'

'Buddy will be just fine, honey,' Mrs Foster said reassuringly. 'Lauren, stop teasing Max and eat some breakfast.'

Lauren sat down and buttered a piece of toast. Max was trying to open a new jar of chocolate spread.

'Come on, Max,' Lauren said impatiently. 'We'll be late.'

Max twisted with all his strength but the lid wouldn't come off.

'Here, let me,' Lauren said, taking it from him and opening it in one go.

'Lauren!' Max protested. 'I wanted to do it! You always interfere!'

'We'd have been here all morning,' Lauren told him.

'That's enough, both of you!' Mrs Foster said, running a hand through her hair. 'Finish your toast and let's go.'

'Hi, Lauren!' Jessica Parker called as Lauren ran into the classroom just before the bell rang.

'Hi,' Lauren said. She still hadn't thought of a plan to help Mel and it was troubling her.

'Samantha and I were looking at ponies for sale in a magazine last night,' Jessica told Lauren. 'There were three that we liked the sound of. We've been trying to get Dad to ring up about them.'

'Any luck?' Lauren asked. She knew how desperate Jessica and her stepsister were to have a pony.

Jessica sighed. 'No. Dad says we've got to wait until the summer holidays.'

Just then, Mel hurried into the classroom.

'Hi,' Lauren said.

'Hello,' Mel replied. Lauren noticed

that her voice was much quieter than
usual.

Before they could say anything else,
the bell rang and Mr Noland came into
the classroom. 'Quiet, please!' he said,
clapping his hands.

As Mr Noland took the register,
Lauren watched Mel. She was looking
pale and unhappy.

'OK, everyone, maths books out,
please,' Mr Noland said as he put the
register away. 'I'd like you to work
through exercise three on page twenty-
two.'

They fetched their maths books and
quiet fell as everyone began working.
Lauren could see that Mel was staring at

the page of fractions, a panicky look on
her face.

'Are you stuck?' Lauren whispered to
her. 'I can help if you like.'

'No . . . no, I'm just thinking,' Mel
replied as she hastily scribbled down an
answer.

Lauren wracked her brains. She wanted to help Mel, but how?

'You don't seem to have done very much, Lauren.' Mr Noland's voice behind her made Lauren jump. 'Do you need some help?'

Lauren looked up guiltily. 'No, I'm fine . . .' she started to say but then she stopped. She'd had an idea. 'Actually, I do need help, please,' she said quickly. 'I'm confused.'

Mr Noland looked surprised. 'But you've been managing fractions OK all week. What seems to be the problem?' He leaned over her desk. 'All you have to do is put the fractions in order, smallest first. You need to consider both the denominator and the numerator –'

'The numerator is the number on top of the fraction and the denominator is the number on the bottom of the fraction, isn't it?' Lauren said, stopping him before he could race on ahead like he usually did.

'Yes and –'

'A fraction is just a small part of a whole, isn't it, Mr Noland?' Lauren said quickly. 'Like one piece of a whole cake. The denominator – the bottom number – tells you how many pieces the cake has been cut into and the numerator – the top number – tells you how many pieces of cake you have.' She glanced quickly to the side and was relieved to see that Mel was listening.

'Yes, that's right,' said Mr Noland, starting to sound a bit impatient.

'So, if the fraction is one third – one over three – the denominator is three which means the cake has been cut into three pieces,' she went on.

'Yes,' Mr Noland replied. 'And if you see the fraction one fifth – one over five – the denominator is . . .?'

Before Lauren could answer, Mel spoke up. 'Five?'

Lauren and Mr Noland looked round.

'That's right, Mel,' Mr Noland said.

'Which means the cake has been cut into five pieces. And the fraction one tenth would mean the cake had been cut

into ten pieces,' Mel said, her eyes starting
to light up. 'One fifth is bigger than one
tenth because if you cut a cake into five
pieces, each slice of the cake is bigger
than if you'd cut it into ten pieces.'

'That's right,' Mr Noland said to her.

Mel's eyes were shining. 'It suddenly all makes sense.'

'Well, that's great,' Mr Noland said. 'How about you, Lauren? Do you understand now?'

'Me?' Lauren caught herself. 'Oh, yes. Thank you, Mr Noland.'

Mr Noland smiled. 'Well, I'm glad you're happier.'

Lauren looked at the relief on Mel's face and smiled. 'Yes,' she said, feeling warm inside. 'I'm much happier now!'

Lauren was still glowing when she got home after school. 'You should have seen Mel's face when she finally worked out fractions,' she told Twilight as she groomed him before tacking him up to take him out on a ride with Mel and her pony, Shadow. 'She looked so relieved.'

Twilight snorted. When he was a pony he couldn't talk to her, but Lauren knew he understood every word she said.

'It kind of made me think,' Lauren said as she cleaned out the curry-comb. 'I know we try and help people when they've got big problems – like helping Jessica when she was really upset about her dad getting remarried, but couldn't we also use your powers to help those with smaller problems too? Sometimes people get almost as upset over something little as over something big.'

She looked at Twilight. He looked as though he was listening hard. 'What do you think?'

Twilight nodded his head.

Lauren hugged him. 'It'll be evening soon,' she whispered. 'We can talk properly then.'

Three

Lauren was untacking Twilight after her ride with Mel when Buddy and Max came charging down the path that led from the house to the paddock.

'We've been at obedience class,' Max burst out. 'Buddy was brilliant! The teacher said he was the best puppy there!'

'That's great,' Lauren said, smiling.

'He learned to sit and lie down and

stay,' said Max. 'Watch!' Taking a handful
of dog treats out of his pocket, Max
called Buddy. 'Buddy! Here, boy!'

Buddy trotted over. 'Sit!' Max said
firmly, holding the treat above Buddy's
head.

To Lauren's amazement, Buddy sat.

'And lie down,' Max said, lowering the
treat.

Buddy did as he was told. 'Now stay,'
Max said. He walked once round Buddy
and then gave him the treat. 'Good boy!'
he cried. 'You did it!'

'Wow,' Lauren said, impressed.

'I can't wait until tomorrow's class,'
Max said happily. 'We're going to learn
how to get the puppies to walk on a

lead. Here, boy,' he called to Buddy, who was snuffling happily in Twilight's grooming kit. 'Let's practise.'

'Maybe it would be best to give Buddy a rest,' Lauren suggested. 'Before he gets tired of learning. We could play hide and seek.'

It was a game that she and Max had just taught Buddy. One of them held the puppy while the other went and hid and then Buddy found them.

'OK,' Max said.

Lauren turned Twilight out in the paddock and then she and Max took it in turns to hide. Buddy found them every time. It was great fun and even Twilight stopped grazing to look.

'Twilight's watching us!' Max
exclaimed, as he tried to push Buddy off
his tummy. 'Buddy! Get off!' he cried as
Buddy licked his nose.

Twilight whinnied. Lauren smiled. It
sounded almost as though he were
laughing.

★

'I'm just going out to see Twilight, Mum,' Lauren said, pulling her trainers on after supper.

'OK, honey,' Mrs Foster replied. She stood up and looked over to where Max was playing with Buddy. 'Come on, Max, time for your bath.'

Lauren ran down to the paddock. She couldn't wait to find out what Twilight thought of her plan about helping people with little problems as well as big.

'So, what do you think?' she asked as soon as he was a unicorn again.

'It's a good idea,' Twilight answered. 'The more people we can help, the better.'

Lauren grinned in delight. 'I was hoping you'd say that!'

'There are some rocks of rose quartz over there,' Twilight said, nodding in the direction of a cluster of trees at the end of his paddock. 'We could check who needs help right now.'

'OK!' Lauren mounted and they cantered down the paddock. Not for the first time, Lauren felt thankful that Twilight's paddock was well hidden from the house. She and Twilight should be safe in the shadow of the trees.

'There they are,' Twilight said, pointing his horn at several small boulders under an oak tree.

'Let's see Mel first,' Lauren said eagerly.

Within a few seconds, a picture had appeared in the rock, showing Mel snuggled up to her mum on the sofa.

'She looks much happier,' Twilight said, pleased.

Lauren nodded. 'OK, let's try Jessica.'

Twilight said Jessica's name and the picture changed. Jessica was sitting in the kitchen talking to her dad. She was frowning. Lauren leaned forward to find out why Jessica was looking so miserable.

'But I really wanted a pony, Dad,' Jessica was saying.

'It'll be easier to find one in the summer holidays,' Mr Parker replied. 'We'll have more time.'

Lauren sighed. She knew Jessica

wanted a pony right now, but she didn't
see how she and Twilight could help with
that. She was about to ask him to look at
someone else when Jessica said something
that caught her attention.

'But I get left out, Dad,' she said.
'Lauren and Mel meet after school to go
riding together and I can't join in. Like
this afternoon, they went riding together
and I couldn't go with them.'

Lauren sat back. 'Did you hear that?'

Twilight nodded. 'It can't be much fun
for Jessica seeing you and Mel riding
together.' He shook his mane. 'But it's
easy to solve. When you and Mel next
meet up, ask Jessica to join you. You can
take it in turns to ride me and Shadow.'

'Good idea,' Lauren said. Fired up by
thinking how easy it would be to solve
Jessica's unhappiness, she looked at the
rock again. 'OK, let's see if anyone else in
my class is unhappy.' She started
suggesting different names. A little
niggling feeling ran through her. She
knew she shouldn't really be listening in
on other people's conversations. Still, it
was for the best, wasn't it? It was so she
could help them.

Lauren got so engrossed in seeing the
other kids from her class going about
their everyday lives – watching TV,
reading, doing homework – that she
almost forgot that she was supposed to be
looking for someone who was unhappy.

She was relieved – everyone seemed to
be doing just fine. She glanced at her
watch. 'I hadn't realized it was so late.'
She stood up. 'We've only got ten
minutes before I have to go in. We'll just
have time to have a very quick fly-round
tonight.'

'Let's go then,' Twilight said, touching his horn to the rock and making the picture disappear. Lauren mounted and held on to his mane.

Twilight started to trot forward, but then suddenly stopped. 'I feel tired,' he said, sounding surprised.

'Tired?' Lauren echoed.

'Yes, sort of achy but . . . but . . .' Twilight looked confused. 'It's strange – I never normally feel tired when I'm a unicorn.'

'We don't have to fly tonight,' Lauren said, concerned. 'Maybe you're not well.'

'No, I'll be fine,' Twilight replied bravely. 'Let's try again.' He trotted forward and this time took off into the sky. Lauren felt the cool wind streaming against her face. She leaned forward. They were flying again!

But soon she started to feel worried. Twilight seemed to be going slower than usual. Normally he galloped and swooped lightly and easily, but tonight his movements felt heavy and slow.

'Are you OK?' she asked.

'I . . . I feel a little strange,' Twilight replied.

'Let's go down,' Lauren said quickly.

Twilight didn't argue. Turning, he flew back to the paddock.

As he landed, Lauren slid off his back. He was breathing heavily. 'What's wrong?' she asked.

'I don't know,' he answered.

'Maybe you're coming down with some sort of bug,' Lauren said anxiously. 'Shall I get Dad to call the vet?'

Twilight shook his head. 'I don't feel ill. Just tired. I'll probably be better in the morning.'

'I'll turn you back into a pony and make you a warm bran mash,' Lauren said. 'That might help.'

Twilight nodded and Lauren said the Undoing Spell. Then, going to the feed room, she put several scoops of bran, a handful of oats and some salt into a bucket and added hot water. Mixing it all up, she carried it back to Twilight. 'Here, boy, eat this.'

Twilight whickered gratefully and plunged his nose into the bucket.

As he ate, Lauren kissed his head. *Oh, Twilight,* she thought, biting her lip, *please be OK.*

Four

Lauren didn't sleep well that night. As soon as she woke up, she looked out of her window. Twilight was standing by the gate. Pulling on her clothes, Lauren hurried outside.

'Are you feeling better now?' she asked.

To her relief, Twilight nodded.

Lauren rubbed his forehead. 'I've been so worried,' she told him softly.

'I don't think I could bear you to be ill.'

'Do you want to go for a ride this evening?' Mel asked Lauren as they got their books out that morning.

'Yes – if Twilight's OK,' Lauren replied.

'What's the matter with him?' Jessica asked, looking concerned.

'He didn't seem very well last night,' Lauren said. 'He was tired.'

'Maybe he's got a cold,' Mel suggested. 'Shadow sometimes gets them. They make him a bit quiet, but they're not serious. So, do you want to meet up?' she asked. 'We could ride at mine instead of going out, then, if Twilight seems tired, you can always go home.'

'OK,' Lauren replied. She happened to glance at Jessica and caught a look of unhappiness fleeting across her face. 'Hey, Jess,' Lauren said quickly, 'why don't you meet us as well? We can take it in turns to ride.'

'Yeah,' Mel said, looking at Jessica. 'That's a great idea.'

'Really? Are you sure you don't mind?' Jessica said hesitantly.

'Of course not,' Lauren told her and Mel shook her head.

'OK then,' Jessica said, smiling. 'Thanks. I'll see if Dad will drop me off.'

To Lauren's relief, Twilight seemed to be back to his normal self when she got home from school that afternoon. He whinnied when he saw her coming.

'Do you feel well enough to go round to Mel's?' she asked him.

Twilight nodded. Feeling much happier, Lauren groomed him and saddled up.

Jessica was already at Mel's house when Lauren and Twilight arrived and the three girls had lots of fun timing themselves as they took it in turns to ride Shadow and Twilight around an obstacle course in Shadow's paddock.

'I've had a great time,' Jessica said happily as they let the ponies graze afterwards while they ate home-made cookies.

'We'll have to do this again,' Lauren said. 'It's more fun when there are three of us.'

'Yeah, definitely,' Mel said. 'Until you get your own pony, you can ride Shadow as much as you like, Jess.'

'And Twilight,' Lauren said.

Jessica's eyes shone happily. 'Thanks, guys. You're the best friends ever!'

'Jessica really enjoyed herself today,' Lauren said to Twilight that night after she had turned him into a unicorn.

'I'm glad we found out that she was upset,' Twilight said.

Lauren nodded. 'Let's have a look and see if there's anyone else who needs our help.'

They went down to the end of the field where the rose-quartz rocks were. The first person Lauren and Twilight saw was a boy in her class, David Andrews, with his father.

'They look like they're arguing,' Lauren

said, leaning closer to the rock.

'I'm not going to wear them!' David
was saying.

'Yes, you are,' his dad replied firmly.
'And I've written to Mr Noland asking
him to make sure that you do.'

'Dad!' David cried.

'It's for the best,' his dad said. He shook
his head. 'David, lots of people wear
glasses . . .'

Lauren looked at Twilight. 'Glasses!' she
exclaimed. 'That's all that's upsetting
David – he's got to wear glasses.'

'Well, if you tell him how good his
glasses look, it might help,' Twilight
suggested.

'It's worth a try,' Lauren agreed. 'Come

on, let's look at some other people.'

Most of the other kids seemed happy enough, apart from Joanne Bailey. Joanne sat at the table next to Lauren and she was miserable because her computer had broken down. She couldn't do the geography research that Mr Noland had asked them to do by the next day.

'I can easily help with that,' Lauren said. 'I'll print out some extra research from the Internet and take it in tomorrow for Joanne to use —'

'Lauren,' Twilight interrupted. 'I . . . I feel strange again.'

Lauren looked at him in concern. 'It's my fault. I shouldn't have made you do that obstacle course at Mel's.'

'But I was feeling all right then,'
Twilight said. 'It's just now – I feel tired
all of a sudden.' He shook his head
wearily. 'Can we stop doing the magic
now? I think I'd better change back.'

'Of course,' Lauren said, jumping to
her feet.

Once Twilight was a pony again, he lay down. Lauren watched him, feeling very worried. What was the matter with him? He was never tired or ill. And this was twice now in two days.

'I'll leave my window open tonight,' she whispered. 'Whinny if you want anything and I'll come straight down.'

Twilight snorted softly and closed his eyes.

Lauren kept her window open all night just as she had promised. At six o'clock, she jumped out of bed and crossed the room to look out. But Twilight wasn't by the gate. Lauren felt alarmed. Twilight always stood there in the morning.

Pulling on her jeans, she hurried outside.

As she reached the paddock, she saw Twilight still lying where she had left him. His nose was resting heavily on the ground and his eyes were closed.

'Twilight!' Lauren cried out.

Twilight's ears flickered and he half-raised his head. He looked exhausted.

Lauren scrambled over the gate and raced across the grass. Throwing herself down on the ground beside him, she touched his neck. 'Twilight!' she gasped. 'What's the matter? You look really ill!'

Twilight snorted weakly.

'I'm going to get Dad!' Lauren said, jumping to her feet. 'Don't worry, Twilight. I'll be back as soon as I can.'

Five

Mr Foster was very worried when he saw Twilight. 'I'm going to call the vet,' he said.

As he hurried off, Lauren crouched down beside her pony. 'You're going to be OK,' she told him, her eyes stinging with hot tears. 'We'll find out what's wrong with you, I promise.'

Tony Blackstone, their vet, arrived

within the hour. He took Twilight's temperature and monitored his heart rate, then he ran his hands all over Twilight's body.

'Has Twilight been off-colour for a while?' he asked Lauren.

'He seemed tired the day before yesterday,' she replied, 'but otherwise he's been fine.'

'So he hasn't had a cough, or runny nose, or been restless and wanting to roll?'

'No,' Lauren replied.

Tony continued his examination, but at last he shook his head. 'Well, it's puzzling. If it weren't for the way he's acting, I'd say he seems to be a very healthy pony. I'll take a blood test and see what shows up.

Maybe he's got a virus.'

'Is there anything we can do?' Mr Foster asked.

'Call me if he gets any worse, but otherwise just let him rest. I'll ring you with the test results as soon as I have them.' Tony shot Lauren a comforting glance. 'Don't worry. I'm sure he's going to be just fine.'

Lauren thought about Twilight all the way to school. What if there was something seriously wrong with him? A cold feeling clenched at her heart.

Walking into the cloakroom, she saw Joanne Bailey talking to her friend, Rachel. Lauren suddenly remembered about the extra research that she had printed out. 'Hi,' she said to them, as she put her coat on the peg. 'Did you do the geography homework last night?'

'Yeah,' Rachel replied.

'I couldn't,' Joanne said. 'My computer broke down.'

'I've got some extra if you need some more,' Lauren offered eagerly.

'It's OK, thanks,' Joanne replied. 'Rachel's lent me some of hers.'

'Are you sure?' Lauren asked, taking out the papers. 'I have them right here.'

'No, really, I'm fine,' Joanne said, and turned back to continue her conversation with Rachel.

Feeling disappointed that her plan to help hadn't worked out as she'd hoped, Lauren went into the classroom. As she walked through the door, she saw David talking with a group of his friends. She stopped. David had his new glasses on but, to her relief, his friends didn't seem to be teasing him.

Just then, David glanced up and caught her watching him. 'What are you looking at?' he asked suspiciously.

'Nothing,' Lauren replied.

'It must be your glasses,' one of David's friends sniggered.

'It isn't!' Lauren said quickly, seeing David go red. 'They're . . . they're very nice glasses.'

David's friends burst out laughing.

'Lauren likes you, David!' one of them said.

'Lauren Foster wants to be your girlfriend.'

'No, I don't!' Lauren exclaimed.

She hurried to her desk, her own
cheeks burning. As she went, she could
hear David's friends start to tease him
about how girls really liked boys with
glasses. *Oh, great,* Lauren thought in
dismay. *I haven't helped David at all — in*

fact, it looks like I've made things worse!

To her relief, Mel and Jessica arrived and she didn't have to listen to David's friends any more.

After school, Lauren went straight to see Twilight. To her relief, he whinnied when he saw her and trotted over to the gate. Lauren's heart rose. He looked much happier.

She got out her grooming kit and spent ages brushing him and combing out every tangle in his mane and tail. As she worked, she told him about David and Joanne. 'They didn't seem to need my help,' she said. 'In fact, I think I made things worse for David by saying that his glasses were nice. His friends started teasing him then.' She sighed. 'I wish you could talk back, but I won't turn you into a unicorn tonight. You've got to rest.'

Twilight nuzzled her.

'I'm going to go and get you some carrots,' Lauren said. 'I'll be back in a minute.'

She hurried to the house. Her dad was in the kitchen with Max. They had just got back from dog-training class and Max was putting Buddy's lead away.

Lauren took three carrots from the fridge. Buddy came over to see what she was doing. She patted him. 'How was Buddy's lesson? Is he still top of the class?'

'No,' Max said, stomping over and sitting down. 'No, he isn't.' Buddy tried to put his head on Max's knee, but Max pushed him away.

Mr Foster sighed. 'Buddy wasn't very good today,' he explained to Lauren. 'They were trying to teach the puppies to fetch a toy, but Buddy just kept running off and not coming back.'

Max stared at the floor.

'Don't worry,' Lauren said sympathetically. 'I'm sure Buddy will learn soon.'

'Lauren's right, Max,' Mr Foster said. 'You've got all weekend to teach Buddy how to fetch. There isn't another class until Monday.'

Lauren bent down and stroked the puppy. 'He'll learn to fetch, won't you, Buddy?'

Looking up at her, Buddy wagged his tail.

The next morning, Tony Blackstone came to check on Twilight again. 'Nothing obvious has shown up on the blood test,' he told Lauren and Mr Foster, 'but I'll send it off to the lab for further analysis. Still, I'm sure there's nothing to worry about. He looks better already, don't you, boy?'

Twilight whickered.

Tony smiled. 'You'd almost think he could understand what I was saying.'

Lauren only just managed to hide her grin. *If only he knew!* 'Should he rest today?' she asked.

'Yes, just to be on the safe side,' Tony said.

As Mr Foster walked with the vet back to his car, Max picked up a stick and threw it. 'Go, boy!' he called to Buddy. 'Go fetch!'

Buddy bounded up to the stick and grabbed it.

'That's it! Bring it here, Buddy!' Max called.

Buddy wagged his tail, the stick firmly clenched in his teeth.

'Buddy, come here!' Max said, his voice rising in exasperation. He started to walk

towards the puppy, but Buddy dodged
around Max and gambolled away up the
path.

'Buddy!' Max shouted crossly. 'Come
back!'

But Buddy ignored him and galloped
out of sight.

'You could try keeping him on a lead,'

Lauren suggested as Max stared after him.
'Then he couldn't get away.'

'I *know* how to train him, Lauren,' Max
snapped. 'You don't need to tell me.'

'I was only trying to help,' Lauren told
him.

'Well, I don't need your help!' Max
said. 'I –'

Mrs Foster appeared at the top of the path. 'Max!' she interrupted them. 'Can you go and get your swimming things, please? We don't want to be late.'

Max ran off as Mrs Foster walked down to Lauren. 'Do you want to come into town with us, honey?'

Lauren shook her head. 'I'll stay here with Twilight.'

'OK,' her mum said. 'Dad's around. If you need anything, just ask.'

After her mum and Max had driven away, Lauren groomed Twilight and then set to work cleaning his tack and tidying the tack room. By mid-morning everything was spotless.

Lauren went down to the paddock where Twilight was grazing. She sighed. There wasn't much else she could do. Unless . . .

Lauren looked round. Her dad was out on the farm and there was no one else nearby. If she turned Twilight into a unicorn, they could at least talk. Maybe they could even look to see if there were some more people to help. That wouldn't be too tiring. All he'd have to do was touch his horn to a rock.

She led Twilight to the shadow of the trees and said the magic words.

'So, how are you feeling?' she asked as soon as Twilight was a unicorn again.

'Not too bad,' Twilight answered. 'Just a

bit weak and . . .' He pawed at the ground
with his hoof. 'Anyway, I'm feeling better
than I did yesterday.'

'I was so frightened,' Lauren said. 'I
thought you were terribly ill.' She looked
towards the bottom of the field. 'Can we
go and use your magic powers? I want to
see if there's anyone else I can help.' She
sighed. 'I didn't exactly do that well with
David and Joanne yesterday.'

'At least you tried,' Twilight said
reassuringly.

'I guess,' Lauren said as they went over
to one of the rocks.

'When will your mum and Max be
back?' Twilight asked.

'Probably not for ages yet,' Lauren

replied. 'But we could check and see where they are just to be on the safe side.'

Twilight nodded and, touching his horn to a rock, he murmured, 'Mrs Foster and Max.'

The picture in the rock showed Mrs Foster and Max having a drink in town. Lauren leaned closer. 'I'm never going to get Buddy to fetch,' Max was saying.

'Oh, Max!' Mrs Foster said. 'You've only been trying for one day. Just be patient.'

'Poor Max,' Lauren said to Twilight. 'He's really unhappy that Buddy won't –' She broke off. 'I've had an idea!' she said, her eyes widening. 'Why don't I teach

Buddy to fetch? Just think how pleased
Max would be to get back and find that
Buddy could do it after all!'

Twilight didn't answer. He was rubbing
his head against his leg as if it hurt.

Lauren looked at him in concern. 'Are
you OK?'

'I'm feeling strange,' Twilight replied
weakly. 'I think I need to rest.'

'I'll turn you back,' Lauren said
immediately.

As soon as Twilight was a pony again
he sighed and half-shut his eyes.

Lauren stroked his face. 'Do you want
anything?'

Twilight shook his head.

'OK,' Lauren said. 'Well, I'll be by the

stable with Buddy. If you need me, just
whinny.'

She went to find Buddy. The puppy
was asleep in the kitchen. He got up
eagerly when Lauren came in.

'Come on, boy,' Lauren said, taking a
packet of dog treats, a long dog lead and
a toy from the cupboard. 'I'm going to
teach you to fetch.'

Taking Buddy outside, she clipped on
his lead. 'I'm going to throw this toy,' she
told him. 'And I want you to bring it
back.'

Buddy woofed in excitement as he
looked at the orange plastic duck in her
hand.

'Go on then, boy,' Lauren said,

throwing the
toy. 'Go fetch!'

Buddy raced after the
duck, grabbed it and then, just as he had
done with Max, he started to bound
away. But this time, the lead pulled him
up short. He stopped in surprise and
shook his head.

Lauren held out a dog treat. 'Here, boy,'
she encouraged.

Buddy looked at her and tried to back off but the lead held him tight.

Lauren waved the dog treat. 'Come on, Buddy.'

Buddy hesitated for a moment and then seemed to make up his mind. Still holding the toy, he trotted over to her.

'Good boy!' Lauren cried as he dropped the plastic duck and eagerly gobbled up the treat. She made a fuss of him and then stood up. 'OK. Let's try that again.'

Twenty minutes later, Buddy had got the hang of fetching the toy. As soon as he picked it up, he carried it back to Lauren, knowing that a treat was waiting for him.

'You are *such* a clever boy,' Lauren
praised him after he had done it without
the lead attached. 'Max is going to be so
pleased!'

Buddy wagged his tail and, leaving him
to play, Lauren went back to check on
Twilight.

He was lying down in the paddock.
Lauren knelt down beside him. 'Twilight?
How are you feeling? Shall I get Dad to
call the vet?'

Twilight shook his head and rested his
muzzle on her knees.

'Oh, Twilight,' Lauren said. 'I wish I
knew what the matter was.' She massaged
his ears and he sighed.

❋

Lauren wasn't sure how long she'd been sitting with Twilight when the silence was broken by the sound of Max's voice.

'Buddy! Where are you?' Max came running down the path to the paddock. Buddy woofed in delight and bounded over to say hello.

Seeing Twilight lying down, Max stopped in concern. 'Is Twilight sick again, Lauren?'

Lauren stood up. Her legs felt stiff from sitting on the ground for so long. 'He just seems tired.'

'Poor Twilight,' Max said. 'I hope he gets better soon.' He patted Buddy. 'Come on, Buddy. Now that I'm back I'm going to teach you to fetch.'

Lauren remembered her good news. 'You don't have to,' she said, smiling.

'What do you mean?' Max said in surprise.

'I taught him while you were out. Watch this.' Seeing the toy duck lying by the gate, Lauren picked it up and threw it. 'Fetch, Buddy!'

Buddy trotted over, picked the duck up and brought it back. 'Good boy!' Lauren exclaimed, feeding him a dog treat from her pocket.

She turned to Max, her eyes shining. 'What do you think?'

To her surprise, she saw Max was frowning crossly at her. 'But Buddy's my dog. I wanted to teach him!' he cried.

'I was just trying to help,'
Lauren said.

'No, you weren't.' Max
looked close to tears. 'You just
wanted to show that you
could do it and I
couldn't!'

'Max —' Lauren began.

But Max wouldn't listen. 'You always interfere, Lauren! You always ruin things!' Pushing past her, he ran off into the woods at the side of the paddock.

Lauren watched him go, feeling awful. She wanted Max to be pleased. She hadn't meant to upset him. But now that she thought about it, she could see what he meant. Perhaps training Buddy hadn't been a good idea. How would she feel if someone had done the same thing with Twilight? She wondered whether to go after him, but decided it was best to leave him until he'd calmed down.

With a sigh, she turned and went to find her mum to tell her about Twilight.

★

'I'll call Tony,' Mrs Foster said, looking at
Twilight lying down in his field. 'Have
you been riding this morning?'

'No, we just –' Lauren broke off. 'Well,
we just stayed in the field.'

'So there's no reason why he should be
tired,' Mrs Foster said.

Lauren shook her head. All Twilight
had done that morning was some magic.
A thought struck her and she almost
gasped out loud. *Magic!* Of course! Why
hadn't she thought about it before?

Lauren's thoughts raced. Every time Twilight had started feeling strange, he had been in his unicorn form doing magic. Maybe he had some sort of special unicorn illness. That would explain why Tony Blackstone couldn't find anything wrong with him!

As her mum went back to the house to ring the vet, Lauren ran to Twilight.

'Twilight!' she said urgently.

Twilight looked up.

'I've had an idea. Maybe it's not the pony bit of you that's sick,' she said, 'maybe it's the *unicorn* bit! You always seem to be ill just after we've done some magic.'

Twilight looked thoughtful but Lauren couldn't tell exactly what he was thinking. She was filled with frustration. If only she could turn him into a unicorn and ask him what he thought, but she couldn't. Not in the middle of his field in broad daylight with her mum around. Then she had an idea.

'Maybe my book on unicorns will have something on unicorn illnesses,' she said. 'After all, that's where I found the words for the Turning Spell.'

Twilight bowed his head, as if in agreement.

'I'll be back later,' she said, almost running into her mum coming in the opposite direction.

'What's the matter?' her mum said in alarm. 'Has Twilight got worse?'

'No,' Lauren said. 'There's no change in him.'

'Well, I spoke to Tony,' her mum said. 'He's out on call at the moment and can't come over, but he said he'll ring in a few hours and see if there's any improvement.'

Lauren nodded. 'Thanks, Mum.' And before her mum could ask her what she was doing she raced on to the house and up to her bedroom. There she picked up the battered blue book lying by her bed and sat down. Turning to the front page, she scanned down the five chapter headings.

Chapter One:
Noah and the Unicorns
Chapter Two:
Arcadia
Chapter Three:
Unicorn Myths
Chapter Four:
Unicorn Habits
Chapter Five:
Unicorns and Humans

Lauren frowned. None of them seemed
to be about illnesses. She looked at the
list again. She knew the first chapter
about Noah and the unicorns almost by
heart now, but maybe one of the others
might have something useful in them.
Opening the book at the second chapter,
she started to read.

Half an hour later, a knock at the door
made her look up. 'Lauren?' her mum
said, looking round the door. 'Have you
seen Max?'

'No.' Lauren's head was swirling with
unicorn facts. 'No, I haven't.'

'He must be outside somewhere with
Buddy,' Mrs Foster said. 'I'll call him. It'll

be lunchtime in five minutes.'

Lauren nodded. She just had a few more pages to read.

Mrs Foster left and Lauren turned back to the last chapter. She hadn't found out anything about unicorn illnesses and she was starting to feel increasingly desperate. The last chapter was all about what unicorns did on Earth. Lauren skimmed over the words. She knew most of it already. She read the last paragraph.

Magic is a very powerful force. It must be used wisely or it will exact a powerful toll. Only when a unicorn's powers are used to help those who are truly in need, will the unicorn be strengthened and his powers replenished.

Lauren frowned at the words. What did they mean? She thought she understood the last sentence – if Twilight did good, then he would become stronger. Well, that was all right. They'd been doing loads of good recently. He should be extra strong.

'Lauren!' her mum called from downstairs. 'Can you come here, please?'

Lauren sighed and shut the book. She'd found out absolutely nothing about unicorns getting ill. Maybe they *didn't* get sick. Maybe her idea had been wrong after all.

She walked slowly downstairs. As she went into the kitchen, she stopped in surprise. She'd been expecting to see Max and her mum sitting at the table ready to eat lunch. But there was no sign of Max, and her mum was standing by the sink, looking worried.

'I can't find Max anywhere,' Mrs Foster said. 'I've been calling him, but he hasn't come in.'

Lauren frowned. 'Maybe he's playing with Buddy.'

'Buddy's here,' her mum said, pointing under the table.

Lauren's stomach tightened. Max hardly ever went off without his puppy.

'When did you last see him?' Mrs Foster asked her.

'It was just after you got back from swimming,' Lauren replied. Just then, she remembered the argument and her cheeks flushed. 'We had a bit of a fight.'

'What sort of a fight?' her mum asked quickly.

'I'd taught Buddy to fetch while you were out,' Lauren said. 'I was just trying to help but Max got really cross and ran off into the woods. I didn't mean to upset him, Mum.'

'Oh, Lauren,' Mrs Foster sighed. 'I understand, but I can see why Max got angry. It's hard for him being the youngest. Sometimes it must seem to him as if you do everything before him. Training Buddy is the first thing he's ever done on his own.'

'I know, I should have realized,' Lauren said regretfully.

'I'd better call your dad on his mobile phone,' Mrs Foster said. 'Perhaps Max is with him.'

Lauren watched anxiously as her mum made the call. She could tell from her face that it wasn't good news.

Mrs Foster replaced the receiver. 'Your dad hasn't seen Max. He's coming back to help us look.' She twisted her hands together. 'Which way did Max go when he ran off, Lauren?'

'Into the woods,' Lauren replied.

'That must have been about an hour and a half ago,' Mrs Foster said, checking her watch. 'I'll try ringing his friends. Maybe he went to one of their houses. Otherwise we'd better start searching.'

None of Max's friends had seen him, and when Mr Foster got back he and two of the farmhands, Tom and Hank, set out to look in the woods.

'Max could be anywhere,' Mrs Foster

said to Lauren. 'He could still be walking or he might be hiding or . . .' her voice faltered, 'he might be hurt.'

'It'll be OK, Mum,' Lauren said quickly. An idea had come to her.

Mrs Foster nodded and took a deep breath. 'Yes, you're right,' she said, as if she were trying to convince herself. 'It will.' She shook her head. 'Oh, if only we knew which direction he'd gone. I just want him home.'

'I . . . I'm just going to see Twilight,' Lauren said.

Mrs Foster nodded distractedly. 'I'll stay by the phone.'

Lauren ran down to Twilight's field. Twilight had stood up and was by the gate.

'Twilight!' Lauren burst out. 'I know you're not well, but Max has run away and no one knows where he is – I really need your help. Please can I turn you into a unicorn? It would just be for a few minutes so that you can use your magic to see if we can find out where Max is. I wouldn't ask but . . .'

Twilight was already nodding his head up and down.

'Oh, thank you!' Lauren gasped.

Twilight started to trot to the trees. Lauren ran after him. As soon as they reached the safety of the shadows, Lauren said the magic words.

As she spoke the last line of the verse, she tensed expectantly.

There was a pause. For one awful
moment, Lauren thought that the spell
wasn't going to work, but then there was
a weak purple flash and Twilight was
suddenly a unicorn again.

'What happened then?' Lauren gasped.

'I don't know. It felt very strange,' Twilight replied, looking confused.

'I thought you weren't going to change,' Lauren said, her heart pounding.

'Let's not worry about it now,' Twilight said quickly. 'We need to find out where Max is.' He touched his horn to the nearest rose-quartz rock. 'I want to see Max!'

Lauren and Twilight waited. They looked at each other.

Nothing had happened!

CHAPTER

Seven

'It hasn't worked,' Lauren said, looking round. 'Maybe it's the wrong sort of rock. Try that one.' She pointed desperately to another.

Twilight trotted over. 'Max!' he said, touching his horn to the hard surface.

Again, nothing. Lauren looked horrified.

'Your magic's not working!' she exclaimed.

Twilight looked totally bewildered. 'I don't feel right. I feel drained, as if,' he looked at her in alarm, 'as if all my magic's been used up.'

His words sent a shock through Lauren. 'Used up? But it can't be!'

'That's how it feels,' Twilight said.

'But the unicorn book said that when unicorns do good they get stronger and their magic gets replenished,' Lauren said. 'We've been doing lots of good deeds. You should have loads of magic.'

'What did it say *exactly*?' Twilight asked urgently.

Lauren tried to remember. 'It was

something about how a unicorn's magic mustn't be used lightly. I'll go and get it!'

She raced back to the house and returned a few minutes later with the book. 'Here,' she said, and she read out the last paragraph.

Magic is a very powerful force. It must be used wisely or it will exact a powerful toll. Only when a unicorn's powers are used to help those who are truly in need, will the unicorn be strengthened and —

She broke off with a gasp. 'Oh no! That's it!'

'What?' Twilight demanded.

'Don't you see?' Lauren said, pointing to the book. 'We've been trying to help

everyone with all their little everyday
problems, not people who are truly in
need, so your magic hasn't been
strengthened, it's just been used up. A toll
is something you pay; well, maybe you're
having to pay for how we've been using
your magic. Maybe that's why you've
been feeling ill!'

Twilight stared at her. 'You might be
right.'

Tears sprang to Lauren's eyes. 'What are
we going to do? Now we really need
your magic to help find Max, we can't
use it because there's none left.'

Twilight nuzzled her. 'Don't worry. We
can still help to find Max even if we can't
use my magic. There must be another way.'

He pawed at the ground, as if trying to think. A stick cracked beneath his hoof. 'I know what to do!' he said suddenly. 'Get Buddy and see if he can find Max. Pretend it's hide and seek. Buddy is brilliant at that!'

'Of course!' Lauren exclaimed.

'Turn me back into a pony and we can follow him to Max together,' Twilight said.

Lauren looked at Twilight in concern. 'But you're not well. You're too weak.'

'I don't care,' Twilight said, looking determined. 'I want to help you find your brother.'

'Are you sure?' Lauren said.

'Yes,' Twilight insisted. He nudged her with his nose. 'Come on, we're wasting time!'

Lauren didn't argue with him any longer. She turned him back into a pony, then she went into the house to tell her mother her plan, before fetching Buddy.

'We're going to find Max,' she told the

puppy. She saddled Twilight and led him
and Buddy to the place where she had
last seen Max.

'Find Max, boy,' she said to Buddy.
'Good dog. Off you go.'

Buddy put his nose to the ground and
began to snuffle round. Suddenly he
seemed to pick up Max's scent. With a
woof, he bounded up the path and into
the woods. Lauren mounted Twilight and
they trotted after him.

Lauren's heart was beating fast as they
entered the trees. What if this idea didn't
work? What if they all got lost trying to
find Max? She pushed the thoughts out
of her mind and concentrated on
encouraging Buddy.

'That's it!' she called to the puppy. 'Good boy!'

Buddy set off down a narrow trail away from the main path. Lauren had to duck under low-hanging branches as the path twisted and turned. Brambles caught at her jeans.

She frowned as she tried to work out
where they were. They seemed to be
heading in the direction of . . .

The gorge!

'Buddy! Be careful!' she gasped in
alarm. 'The path ends just ahead. It's
dangerous!'

But Buddy started to run even faster.
He disappeared from sight.

Lauren wondered what to do, but Twilight took the decision out of her hands. Breaking into a canter, he set off through the trees after the puppy. Lauren flung herself down against his neck. Clinging to Twilight's mane, she looked ahead as best she could.

Suddenly Lauren heard Buddy bark and then Twilight jerked to a stop. Her breath came in short gasps as she pushed herself upright in the saddle. Buddy was just ahead of them. He was standing beside a faded wooden sign that read:

DANGER
KEEP BACK

Her heart pounding, Lauren dismounted.

Twilight nuzzled her arm and she could tell he was also worried. Slipping the reins over her arms, she walked cautiously forward. She didn't dare walk right to the edge of the gorge in case the crumbling ground gave way. Letting go of Twilight, she dropped to her hands and knees and crawled the last few metres. She felt sick. What was she going to see when she looked over?

'Buddy!' she called as Buddy inched right to the edge. 'Be careful!'

'Lauren!' a faint voice called.

Lauren felt her heart leap. 'Max!' she gasped.

CHAPTER

Eight

Throwing herself on to her stomach, she looked over the edge of the gorge. Max was crouched on a rocky ledge about four metres below the cliff edge. Beneath him, the gorge tumbled away steeply, ending in a pit of rocks and brambles far, far below. His eyes were wide with fear.

'Lauren,' he cried. 'You found me! I

didn't think anyone ever would.'

'Are you OK?' Lauren asked.

'Yes. I was having a look over the side of the gorge and the ground just sort of crumbled,' Max said. 'But I landed on this ledge. I'm OK. I just can't get back up.'

Lauren went cold as she thought about what might have happened if he hadn't landed on the outcrop.

'I'll go and get help!' she said.

'No! Don't leave me!' Max looked terrified.

Lauren looked desperately at her brother. 'I've got to go. I can't reach you.'

'I don't want to stay here alone,' Max said tearfully.

'But you wouldn't be alone,' Lauren

said desperately. 'Buddy's here.'

'Buddy!' Max gasped in delight. Buddy barked, as if in reply.

'Look, I'm going to have to go and get Mum and Dad, Max,' Lauren said. 'Buddy will stay with you.'

Max looked up. 'OK,' he said bravely.

'I'll be back as soon as I can,' Lauren promised.

Edging away from the cliff, she stood up, commanded Buddy to stay and ran to Twilight. 'Quick, Twilight!' she gasped as she mounted. 'We've got to get home!'

'Lauren! Where have you been? I've been out of mind with worry!' Mrs Foster came running down the path as Lauren and Twilight galloped out of the woods towards the farm. 'How could you have – ?'

'Mum! I've found Max,' Lauren interrupted her mother as Twilight slowed to a trot. 'He's stuck in the gorge.'

'Oh my goodness,' Mrs Foster said, going pale. 'The gorge!'

'He's all right,' Lauren said. 'He's on a ledge. Buddy's with him.'

'I'll ring your dad,' Mrs Foster said. 'He's in the woods.' She turned and ran back to the house.

'I'll go back there,' Lauren called after her. 'I told Max I'd get back as quickly as I could.'

Mrs Foster stopped. 'OK,' she agreed. 'If you get there before your dad, then

tell Max that help will be along very
soon.' She ran into the house.

'Are you OK to go back, boy?' Lauren
asked Twilight.

He nodded and swung round, pulling
eagerly at his bit. He suddenly seemed
much livelier, almost as if he had got all his
energy back. Lauren leaned forward and
they cantered back into the woods again.

Lauren reached the gorge just as her dad,
Tom and Hank jumped out of the pick-
up truck.

'It's OK, Max,' she said, crawling to the
edge. 'Dad's coming.'

'Thanks for getting help, Lauren,'
murmured her brother.

'Lauren! Thank heavens you found
him!' Mr Foster said, hurrying to the
edge of the gorge. Lying down on his
stomach, he looked over. 'It's all right,
Max,' he said. 'We'll get you up.'

Lauren watched as Tom and Hank tied one end of a long coil of rope securely around a thick oak tree and then, using it to hold on to, her dad lowered himself over the edge.

'We're ready to come back up,' he called, once he had been down there for a few minutes.

There was a bit of shouting and then Tom and Hank began to pull on the rope. Mr Foster and Max soon scrambled over the edge of the gorge.

Lauren sighed with relief as her dad hugged Max as if he were never going to let him go. 'Oh, Max! Why did you go off like that?' he said.

'I'm sorry.' Max looked close to tears

again. 'I was just cross with Lauren. I'm really sorry, Dad.'

Mr Foster hugged him. 'Just don't do anything like it ever again.'

'I won't,' Max said, as Mr Foster put him down. Max looked at Lauren. 'I'm sorry I got upset with you, Lauren.'

'It's OK. I should have let you teach Buddy to fetch,' Lauren told him.

'I was being silly,' Max said. He looked at the ground. 'I'd . . . I'd like you to help me train Buddy if you want.'

Lauren smiled. 'You don't need me. You're doing fine on your own, Max. Anyway, I don't think Buddy needs much training,' she said, looking at the puppy. 'No dog could be cleverer. He was the one who found you.'

Max crouched down and hugged Buddy. 'Thanks, boy.' Buddy wagged his tail in delight.

'Come on, Max. Let's get you home,' Mr Foster said. 'The pick-up is just through the trees.' He looked at Lauren. 'Will you be OK riding back on your own?'

'I'll be fine,' she said. She waved as her dad, Hank, Tom and Max set off through the shadows. The pick-up started and Lauren listened as it drove away. Once the woods were quiet again, she took off Twilight's bridle and saddle. Then, taking a deep breath, she said the words of the Turning Spell.

Almost before the last word was out
of her mouth, there was a bright purple
flash and Twilight was a unicorn once more.

'Oh, Twilight,' she said, hugging him.
'Thank you for helping me.'

Twilight pushed his nose against her
chest. 'I'm just glad Max is OK,' he said. 'I
wish I could have used my magic to help
you find him more quickly.'

'It doesn't matter now,' Lauren said.
'Your idea to use Buddy was brilliant. If
you hadn't thought of that, Max might
still be stuck. And anyway,' she went on
quickly, 'it wasn't your fault that we
couldn't use magic. It was mine. I was the
one who used it all up by getting you to
look at my friends.'

'You were only trying to help people,' Twilight reminded her.

'I know,' Lauren said. 'But I didn't really need magic for that. I could have seen that Mel was upset about her fractions and I should have realized that Jessica was feeling left out, and the other people I tried to help – Joanne, David, Max – well, they didn't really need my help at all.' She looked down. 'I think I just liked feeling important.'

Twilight nuzzled her. 'Don't feel bad. It turned out all right in the end.'

'Yes,' Lauren said slowly, 'thanks to you. You're the best, Twilight. Even though you were feeling really ill, you still let me ride you so that we could follow Buddy here.' She hugged him. 'How are you feeling now?'

Twilight considered the question. 'All right, actually. I don't feel tired at all.'

'Maybe it's because we've just helped Max,' Lauren suggested. 'Perhaps your powers have come back now that we've actually helped someone truly in need like the book said.'

'I'm sure that's what has happened,' Twilight said, tossing his head, 'because I feel great!' He pranced on the spot. 'Let's go flying, Lauren!'

'But it's not dark enough,' Lauren protested.

'I'll stay in the treetops,' Twilight said. He pushed her with his nose. 'Come on!

I want to fly!'

Lauren couldn't resist. 'OK then!' she said, scrambling on to his back.

'I could always use my magic . . .' Twilight began teasingly.

'Not a chance!' Lauren interrupted him with a grin. 'From now on we only use your magic powers to help people who truly need help. Agreed?'

'Agreed,' Twilight said. He started to trot out of the trees and then he stopped. 'Am I really the best?' he asked, almost shyly.

Lauren nodded as she hugged him. 'The very best,' she smiled.